This book belongs to

Savnnah

Illustrated by Pamela Storey
Original story by Geoffrey Alan
Adapted by Lynne Gibbs

Published in Great Britain by Brimax Publishing Ltd
Appledram Barns, Chichester PO20 7EQ
Published in the US by Byeway Books Inc,
Lenexa KS 66219 Tel 866.4BYEWAY
www.byewaybooks.com

Printed in China

Bramble Bear

Can I Help?

BRIMAX

One day, Bramble Bear watched as his mother baked some cakes.

"Do you need any help to taste the cakes?" asked Bramble, licking his lips.

"Maybe later," smiled Bramble's mother.

"I know! I'll fetch that big bag of flour over to the table," Bramble said to himself. "That will be very helpful."

Bramble stretched out his arms and reached for the big bag of flour. But it was very heavy.

WHUMP! The bag slipped out of Bramble's little paws – and flour flew everywhere in a big, white cloud!

"Oh, dear! What a mess I've made!" sighed Bramble as he sat on the floor. "I really haven't helped at all!"

"Can I help you?" Bramble asked his dad.

"You could dig up some weeds," puffed Dad, rubbing his aching back. "You do know which are weeds, don't you?"

"Yes," said Bramble. "Have a rest for a while and leave everything to me."

"Thank you," said Bramble's dad. "You are such a helpful little bear."

Bramble quickly set to work, digging and raking and tugging at those nasty weeds.

Soon, the wheelbarrow was full.

But when Dad came back outside he gasped, "You've dug up my prize flowers! Now I'll have to plant them all again!"

"I'm sorry," sighed Bramble. "I thought they were weeds."

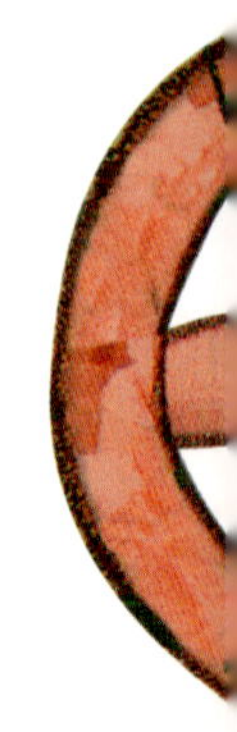

Indoors, Bramble looked around his messy bedroom. "I know how I can be helpful," he smiled. "I'll tidy my room."

First, Bramble put all his clothes away. Then he put his toys in a wooden chest.

"That looks much better," smiled Bramble, feeling very pleased with himself. "Now I'll neatly stack all my books on the shelf."

But Bramble was trying to hold far too many books – and they slipped out of his paws!

As he tried to catch the books, Bramble lost his balance and fell backwards.

CRASH! Bramble broke his bed!

THUMP! THUD! THUMP! Bramble's books landed all around him!

"Don't tell me!" groaned Bramble's dad. "You were just trying to help again!"

"Um, yes," mumbled Bramble.

Leaving his mother to tidy his messy bedroom, while his dad mended the bed, Bramble went for a walk.

Bramble hadn't gone far when he saw two young rabbits pointing up at a tree.

"Our kite is caught on that branch and we can't reach it," said the rabbits.

"I'll get it for you," said Bramble.

Bramble climbed the tree. Higher and higher he went, getting closer and closer to the kite.

Pulling himself along a branch, Bramble called, "I'm nearly there!"

Bramble Bear gave the branch a hard shake – and the kite toppled down.

"Thank you," called the rabbits as they ran off, pulling their kite by its string.

"I was glad to be of help," called Bramble.

But climbing down the tree was much more difficult than Bramble had thought it would be.

"Help! Help! I'm stuck!" called Bramble.

Luckily, the two rabbits heard Bramble's cries and ran to fetch his parents.

"Oh, dear little bear," said Bramble's dad, "whatever have you been up to now?"

"I was trying to be a helpful bear. Now I'm the one who needs help!" sighed Bramble. "Can you fetch a ladder, Dad?"

What are they doing?

Can you point to these pictures as you find them in the story?